For Ramona
who tells stories and makes jokes
and quite possibly sings songs.
S. P.

For my dad and the sisters
Nan, Olive, and Winnie.
Miss you lots.
A. B.

Text copyright © 2001 by Simon Puttock ~ illustrations copyright © 2001 by Alison Bartlett ~ All rights reserved. Published by Scholastic Press, a division of Scholastic Inc., PUBLISHERS SINCE 1920, by arrangement with Mammoth, an imprint of Egmont Children's Books Limited. ~ SCHOLASTIC, SCHOLASTIC PRESS, and associated logos are trademarks and/or registered trademarks of Scholastic Inc. No part of this publication may be reproduced, or stored in a retrieval system, or transmitted in any form or by any means, electronic, mechanical, photocopying, recording, or otherwise, without written permission of the publisher. For information regarding permission, write to Scholastic Inc., Attention: Permissions Department, 555 Broadway, New York, NY 10012. ~ ISBN 0-439-26219-4 ~ Library of Congress Cataloging-in-Publication Data available ~ 12 11 10 9 8 7 6 5 4 3 2 1   01 02 03 04 05 ~ Printed in Dubai. ~ First American edition, September 2001 ~ The display type was set in Coop Flaired. ~ The text type was set in 12-point Keedy Sans Regular.

A Story for Hippo

a book about loss

by Simon Puttock

illustrated by Alison Bartlett

Scholastic Press ~ New York

Hippo was the oldest and wisest of all the animals. She lived on the banks of the wide, blue river and told the most wonderful stories.

Monkey was not as old or as wise as Hippo. To tell the truth, Monkey was a bit of a joker. He could make all the animals laugh with his antics. Monkey lived on the banks of the wide, blue river with Hippo.

Each evening, as the jungle was falling asleep, Hippo told Monkey stories.

"Which story would you like tonight, Monkey? Would you like the one about the three-headed giant?"

"Well . . . perhaps," said Monkey.

"Or the one about the princess and the moon?"

"Well . . . maybe," said Monkey.

"I know," said Hippo. "Would you like the one about you and me?"

"Yes, please!" said Monkey.

"Once upon a time," she began, "there lived a hippo and a monkey."

"Yes," said Monkey, "a big, round hippo, and a middle-sized monkey."

"Exactly," Hippo laughed. "And they were best friends."

"Best, best, best friends," said Monkey.

"And they told stories and ate cabbages."

"And coconuts, too," said Monkey, who loved coconuts.

"And coconuts, too," Hippo agreed. "And they played games—"

"And ran races!" Monkey butted in again.

"Oh, Monkey," Hippo laughed. "This hippo was too old and slowed down to run races. But even so, day by day, they both lived happily ever after."

"Oh, yes," said Monkey contentedly. "That is a good story."

Little Chameleon lived under a leaf on the banks of the wide, blue river. She listened to Hippo's stories and laughed at Monkey's jokes, but she was shy and she stayed beneath her leaf, though she longed to join in. If i were brave enough, she thought, i would sing them a song. Little Chameleon loved to sing.

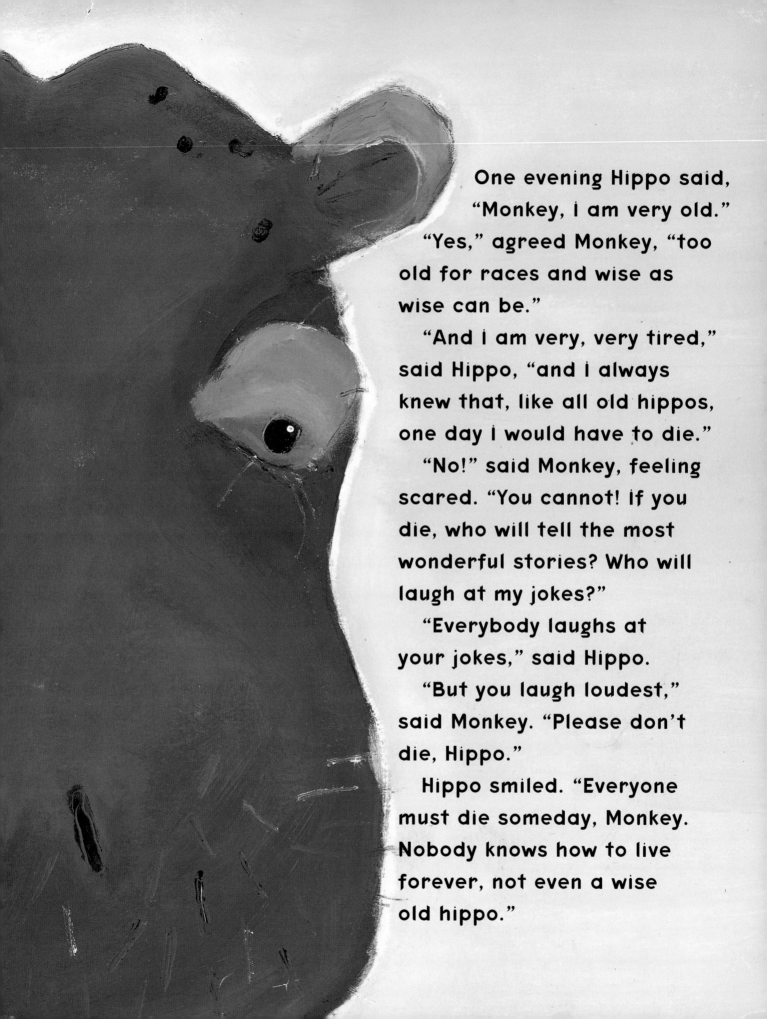

One evening Hippo said, "Monkey, i am very old."

"Yes," agreed Monkey, "too old for races and wise as wise can be."

"And i am very, very tired," said Hippo, "and i always knew that, like all old hippos, one day i would have to die."

"No!" said Monkey, feeling scared. "You cannot! if you die, who will tell the most wonderful stories? Who will laugh at my jokes?"

"Everybody laughs at your jokes," said Hippo.

"But you laugh loudest," said Monkey. "Please don't die, Hippo."

Hippo smiled. "Everyone must die someday, Monkey. Nobody knows how to live forever, not even a wise old hippo."

"Then happily ever after isn't true," said Monkey.
He was angry because Hippo was leaving him.
   "But Monkey," said Hippo, "i have
lived happily ever after. i have
had the best and funniest
friend in all the jungle
and a long and
happy life.

"You will find new friends, tell new jokes, and hear new stories. You will enjoy the days and dream the nights away, and you will live happily ever after, too."

Hippo paused for a moment. "Will you forget me, Monkey?" she asked softly.

"Of course I won't forget you!" shouted Monkey. "You're my best, best, best friend."

"Thank you," said Hippo. "Because that will be part of my happily ever after." Then Hippo went away into the jungle's deepest shade where all the hippos go when it is time for them to die.

Monkey missed Hippo. Day after day he sat by the river and wept. He decided he would never tell jokes again.

The jungle was silent and sad.

Everyone missed Hippo and everyone missed Monkey's antics.

One evening, when the jungle was falling asleep, Little Chameleon crept out from under her leaf. She could not bear to hear Monkey crying anymore.

"Tell me a joke," she said. "i want to laugh."

"Go away," said Monkey. "i can't! i won't!"

"Then tell me a story, please," said Little Chameleon.

"i don't have any stories," said Monkey.

"Yes you do," said Little Chameleon. "You have all the stories Hippo told."

"But they belonged to Hippo," said Monkey, drying his eyes.

"They are your stories now," said Little Chameleon, "and stories need to be told."

"But i miss Hippo," said Monkey.

"i miss her, too," said Little Chameleon. "Please, tell me a story with Hippo inside it."

Monkey sniffed a soggy sniff. "All right, i'll try."

"Once upon a time," he began, "there lived a little chameleon and a monkey."

"That's a good beginning," said Little Chameleon.

"And they missed Hippo very much."

"That's true," said Little Chameleon sadly.

"But Little Chameleon
and Monkey told each
other stories, and
laughed at each
other's jokes,
and . . ." Monkey
paused for a moment.
  "And sang songs," said
Little Chameleon, who
had a beautiful voice
and used to sing the
most wonderful songs
alone beneath
her leaf.

". . . and sang songs," Monkey added. "And after a while they lived happily ever after."

"That is a good story," said Little Chameleon, curling up contentedly on top of her leaf. "Now, tell me another."